Chapter One:
Someone Needs Our Help

From a high building, the Dark Man looks down on the city.

Directly below are the dirty streets of the bad part of the city.

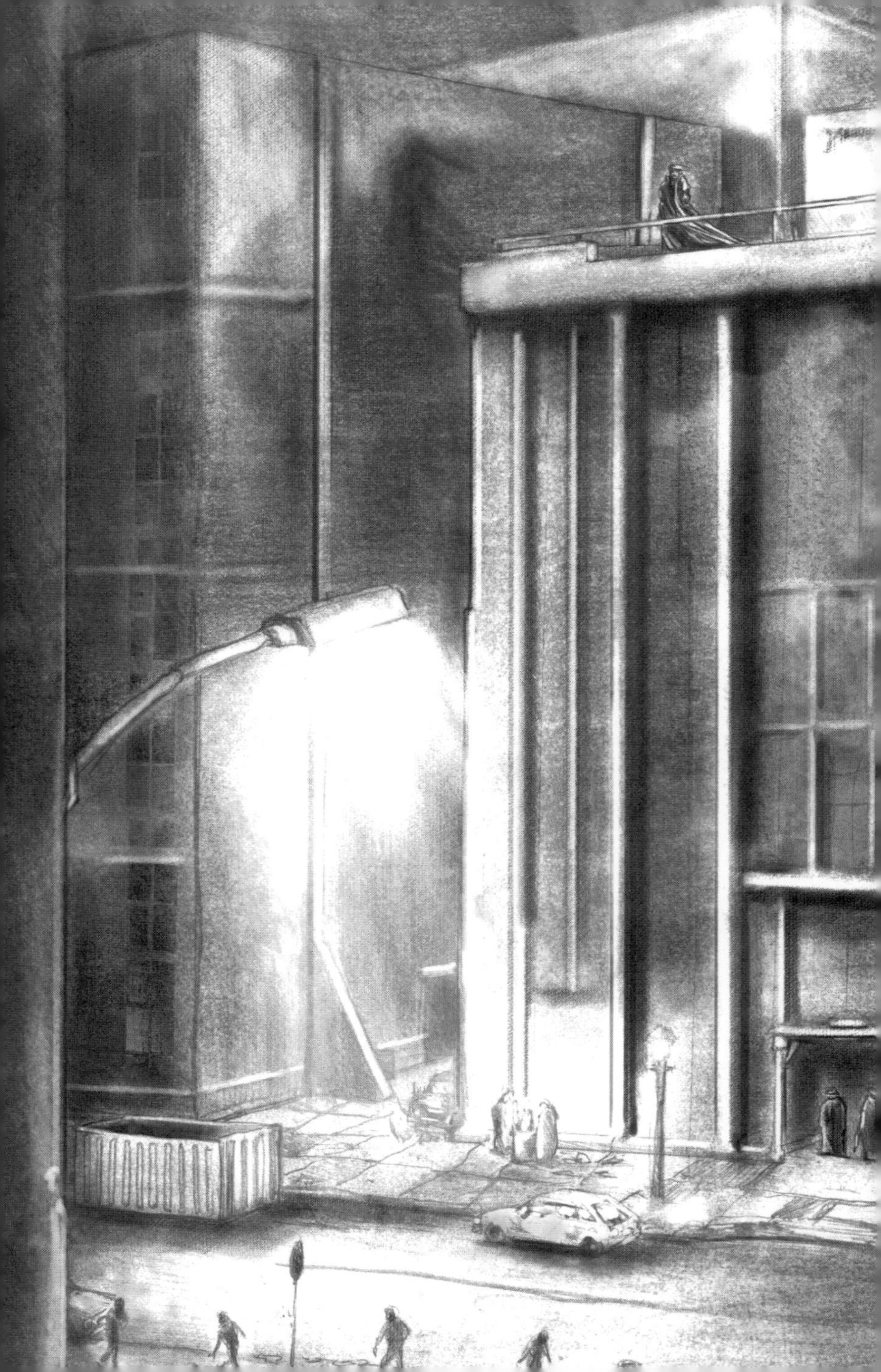

He sees people hurrying.

Groups of young thugs are hiding in doorways.

The Dark Man is sad for the people who have to live here.

He steps back from the ledge and reaches into a coat pocket.

He pulls out a crumpled photo.

The picture is faded, but it is of a smiling girl.

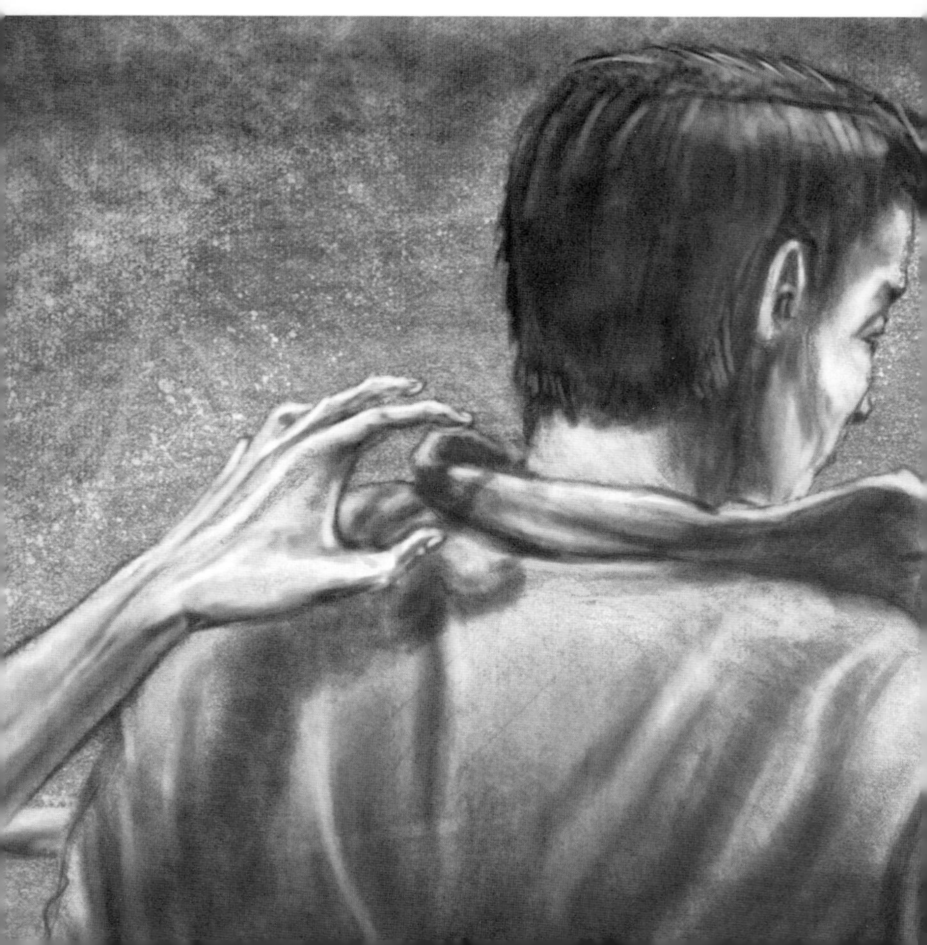

The Dark Man feels a hand placed on his shoulder.

"She is lost, and you know it."

It is the Old Man speaking.

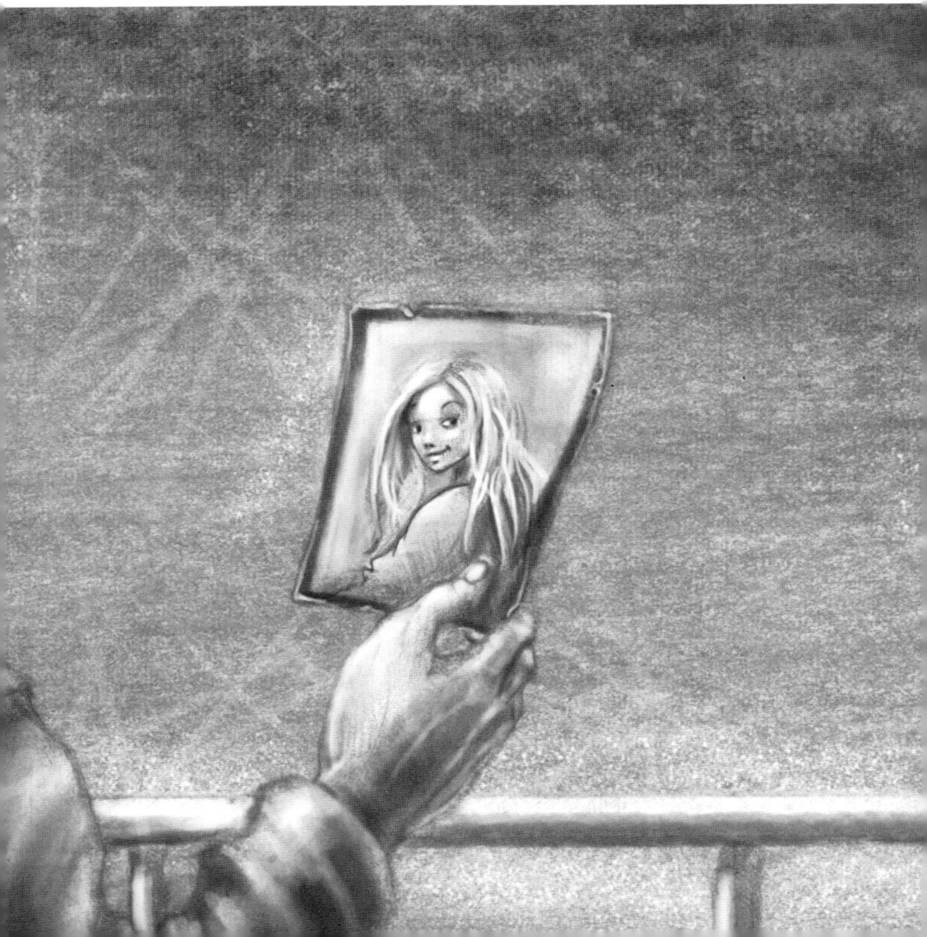

He must have used magic to appear there. Otherwise the Dark Man would have heard him.

The Dark Man puts the photo back in his pocket.

"Why are you here?" he asks.

"There is another who needs our help," the Old Man replies. "Someone who has helped us in the past."

"Who?" the Dark Man asks.

The Old Man waits a moment.

"It is Angela," he says. "The Shadow Masters have her trapped, and we must rescue her."

Chapter Two:
Strange Magic

The Dark Man's eyes narrow.

"Angela is a killer," he says. "The streets are not safe when she walks at night."

The Old Man nods.

"But she has the gift of second sight. Sometimes she can see things that even we cannot."

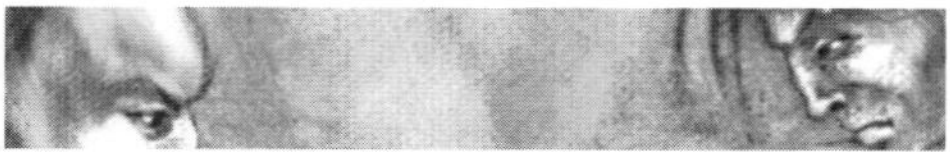

The Dark Man remembers the time when Angela's power had shown him where to find the Golden Cup.

But he also remembers the screams of the young boys from that night.

The thought makes him shiver.

"She is held inside a glass tower in the good part of the city," the Old Man says.

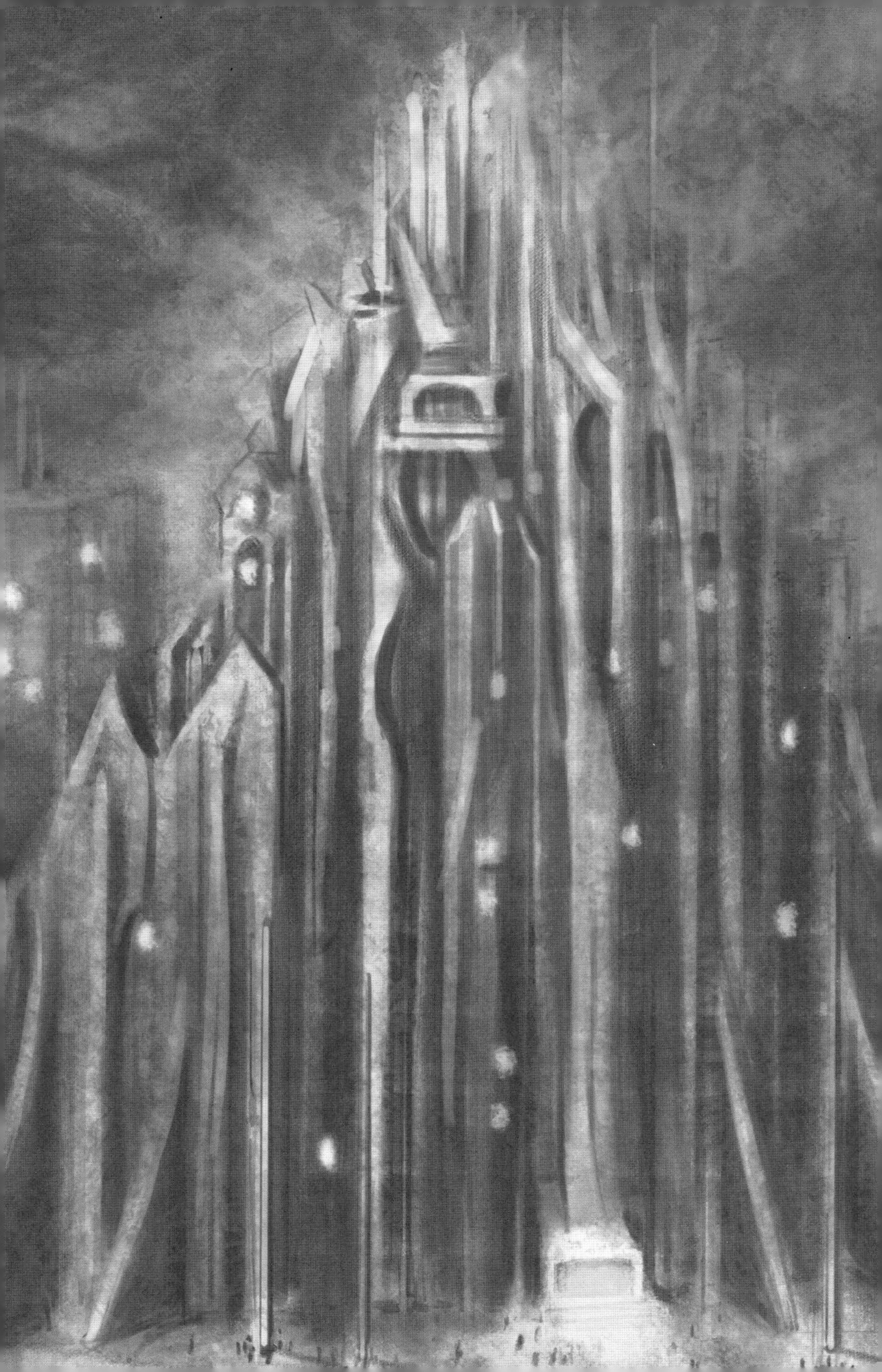

"But right now it is the middle of the day," the Dark Man says. "The darkness of night is a long way away. Why can't you rescue her?"

The Old Man looks long and hard at the Dark Man.

"The Shadow Masters have used a strange magic that turns daylight into darkness."

Now the Dark Man understands. Only he has power in the darkness.

The Old Man takes the Dark Man's hand.

"Close your eyes," he says, "and let your thoughts slip away."

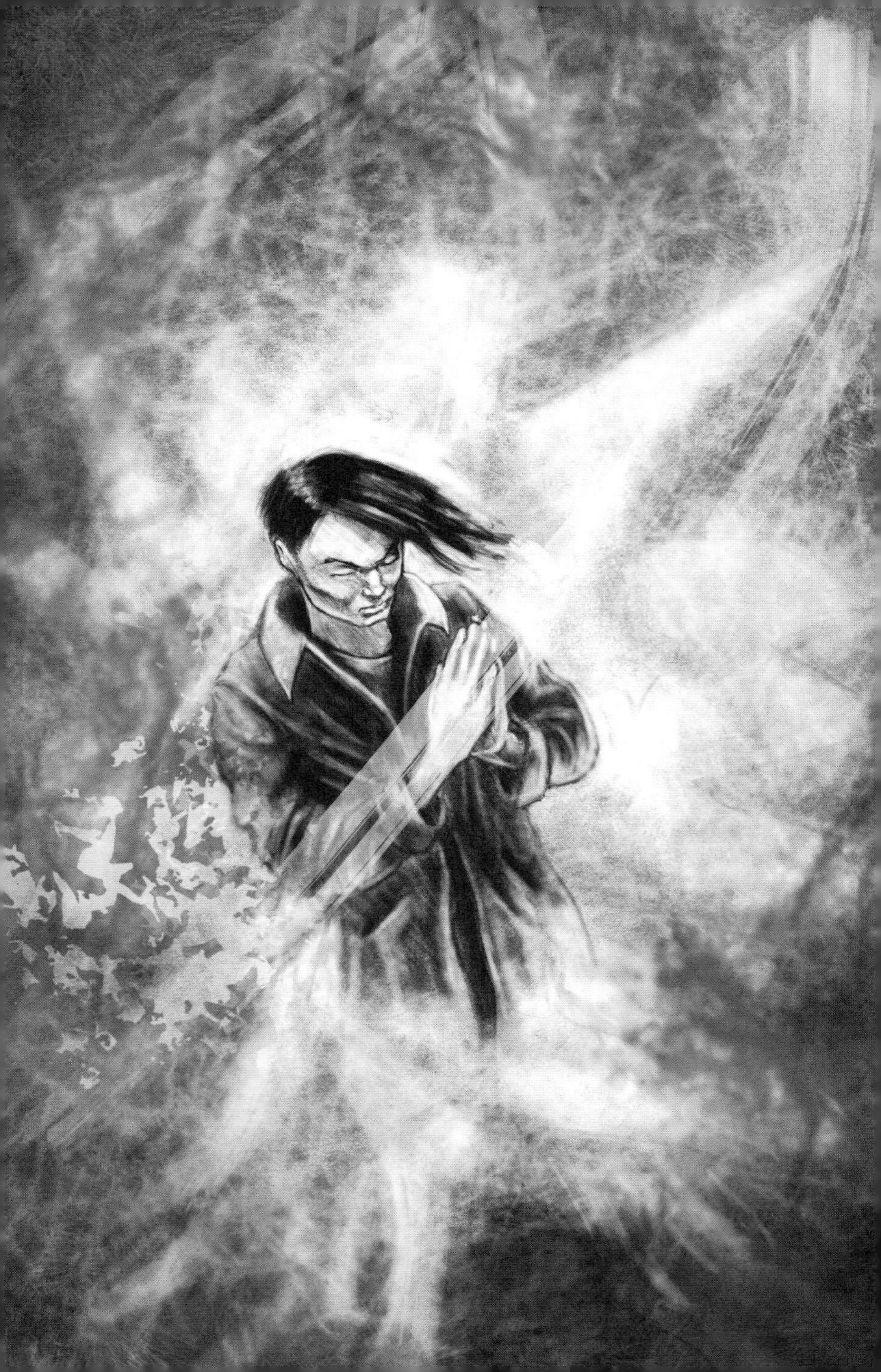

Behind his closed eyes, the Dark Man is aware of a bright flash of light.

When he opens them, he is in the good part of the city.

He is standing before a huge, round glass tower.

The Old Man is not there. It does not matter.

He knows that this is where Angela is held.

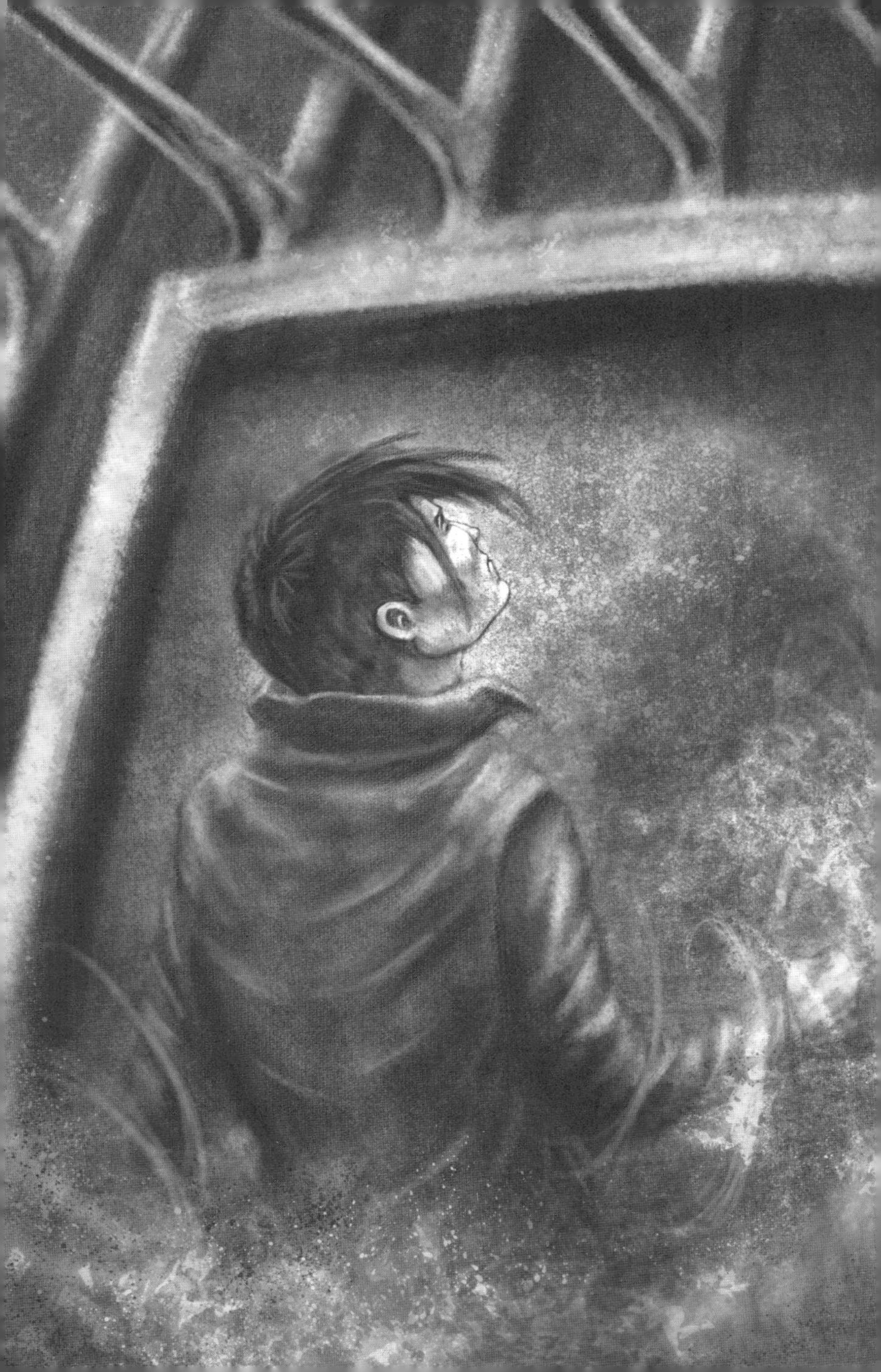

Chapter Three:
The Boy

The Dark Man goes into the building.

There are many people around.

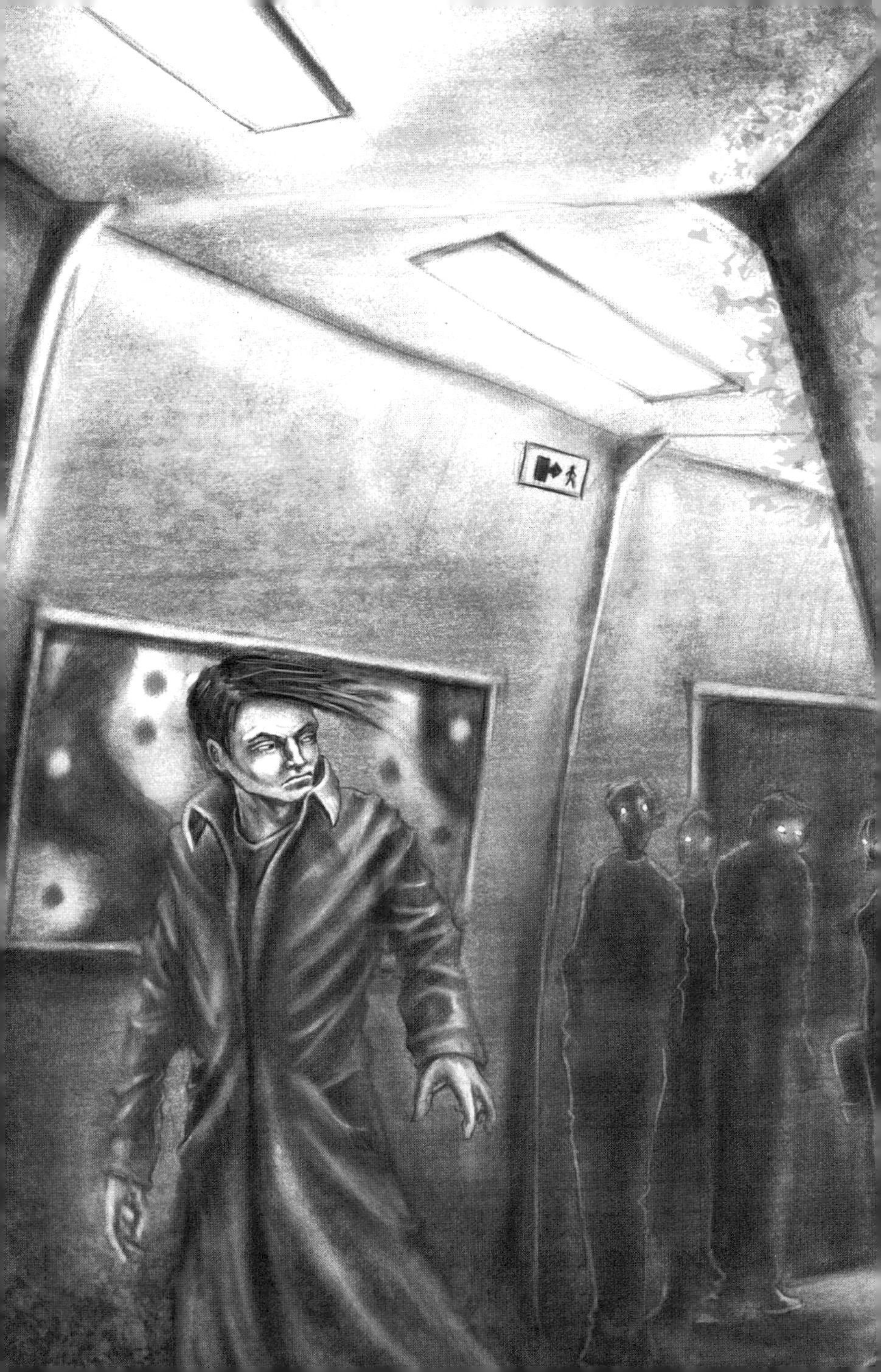

A security guard calls out to him.

"What are you doing here?" the security guard asks.

The Dark Man stares into his eyes. "I belong here," he says.

The security guard seems to be in a trance.

"Yes," he says, "you belong here."

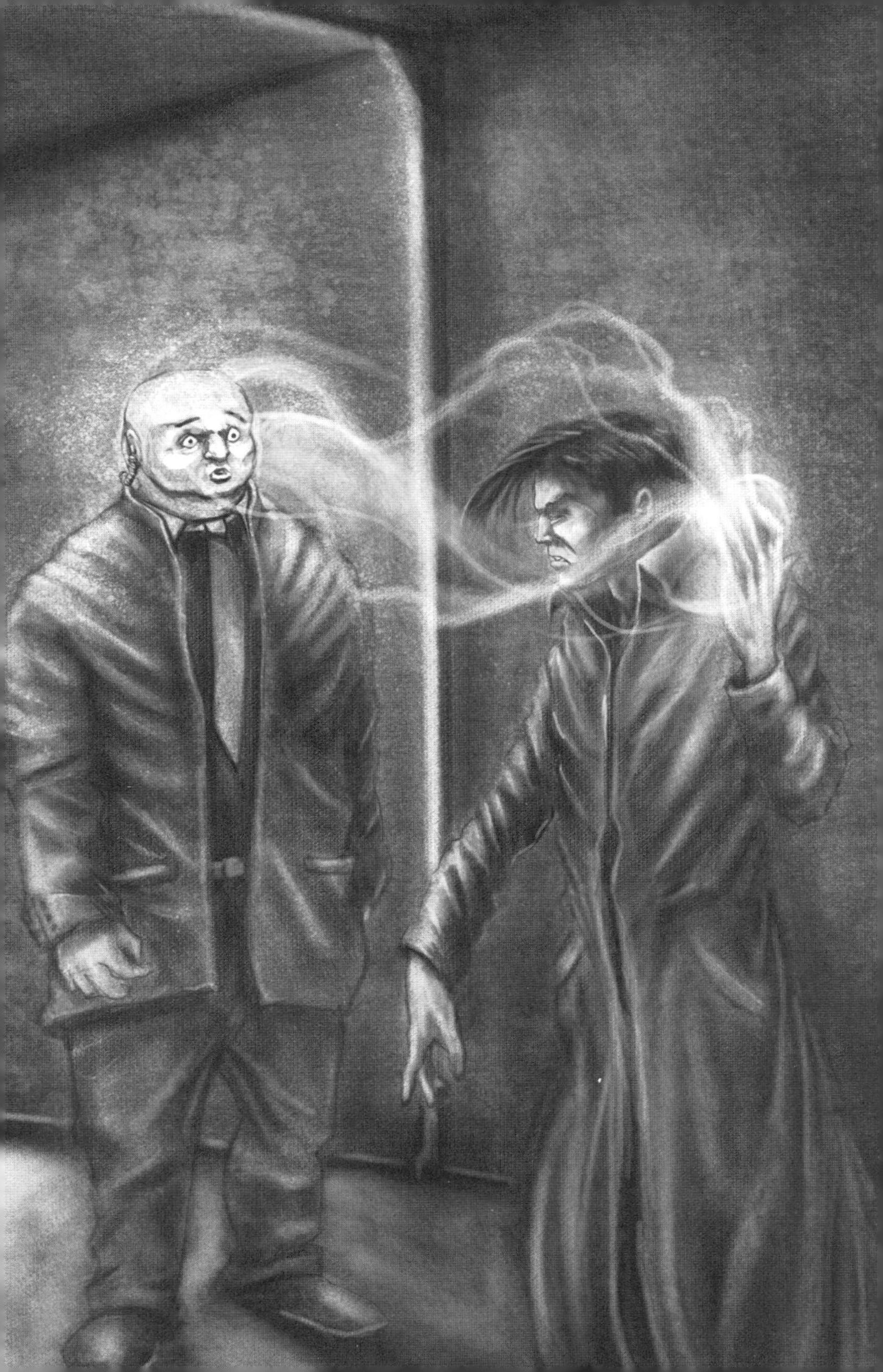

The Dark Man walks over to the elevators.

He will start with the top floor and try to find Angela.

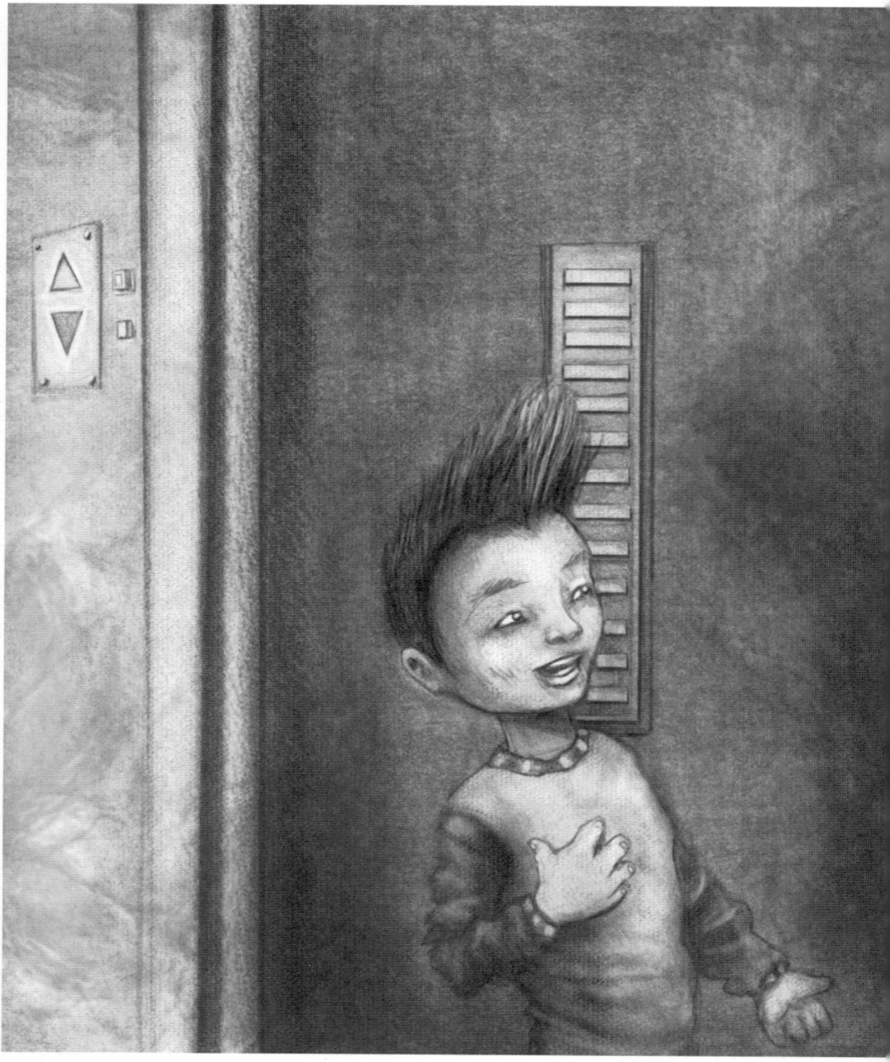

As he steps into an empty elevator, a young boy slips inside with him.

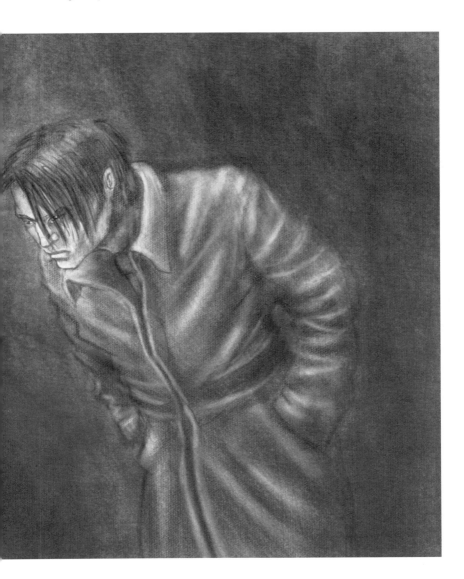

The boy smiles at the Dark Man.

"I can find the room where they are holding her," the boy says.

"Did the Old Man send you?" the Dark Man asks.

The boy nods.

"How can you find her?"

"Because of the dark," the boy says. "I am afraid of the dark."

"Fine," the Dark Man says. "We will start on the top floor."

"No!" the boy shouts. "Two floors down from there."

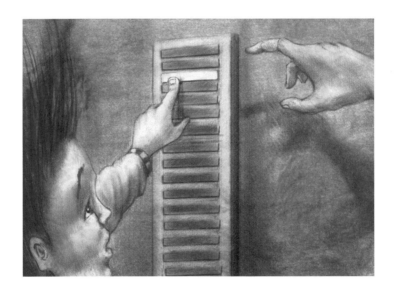

"How do you know?" the Dark Man asks.

"Because that is where I feel most afraid," the boy tells him.

There are lots of twisting corridors.

It is light because the building is made of glass.

Suddenly, the boy stops.

"Around the corner," the boy says. "I'll wait here."

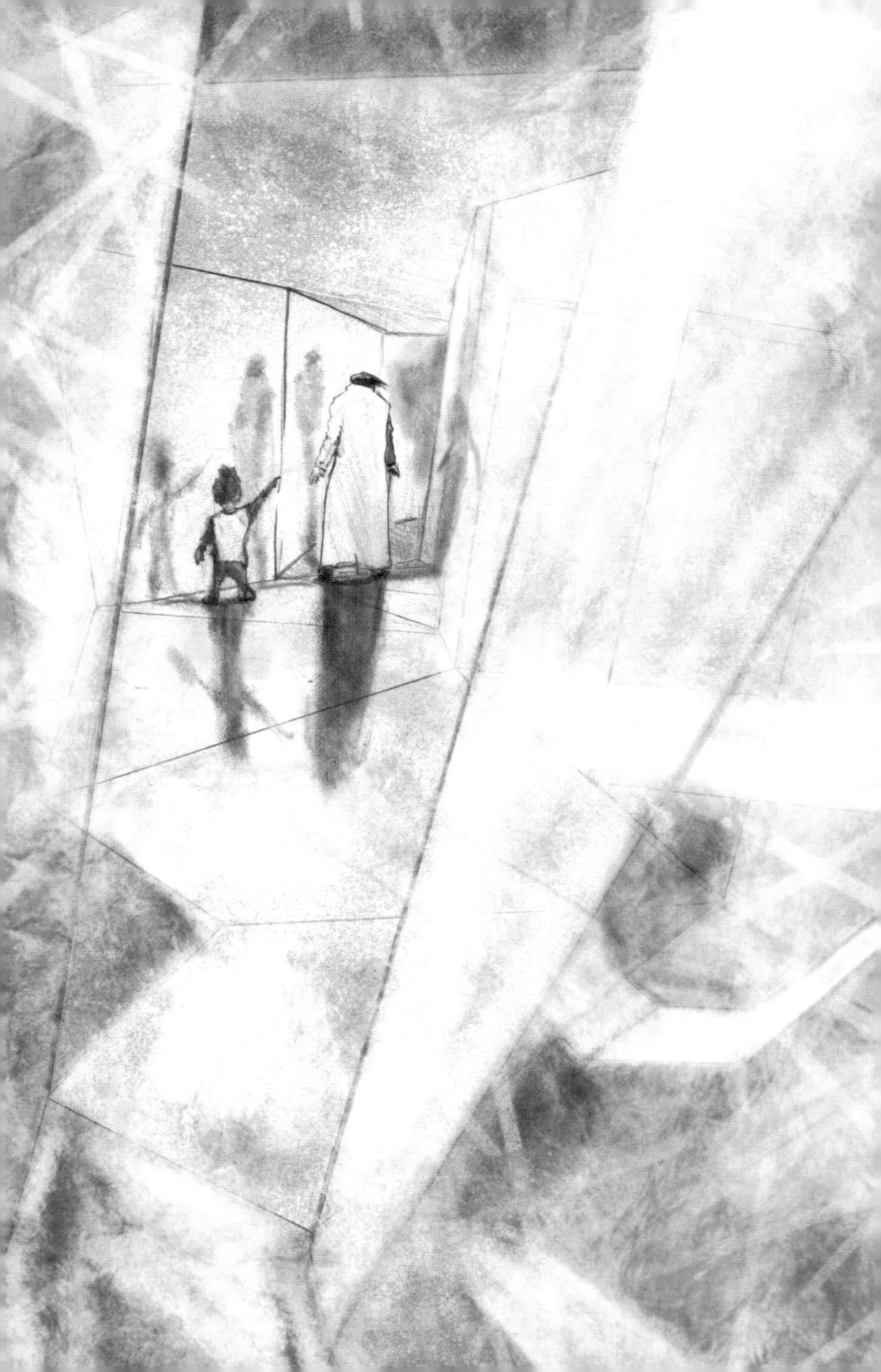

The Dark Man notices that it is not as light here as it should be. The light is gloomy.

"Stay here," he says, and then he steps around the corner.

Strangely, he can see the sun through the glass walls of the building, but it is getting darker as he moves down the corridor.

He has to feel his way along the wall.

Chapter Four:
Living Darkness

His hand touches a door handle.

Slowly, he opens the door and steps into the room. It is pitch-black.

But worse than that, the darkness seems to be alive. It seems to move.

It feels as if it is trying to slip behind his eyelids.

He has to use his hands to brush it away from his face.

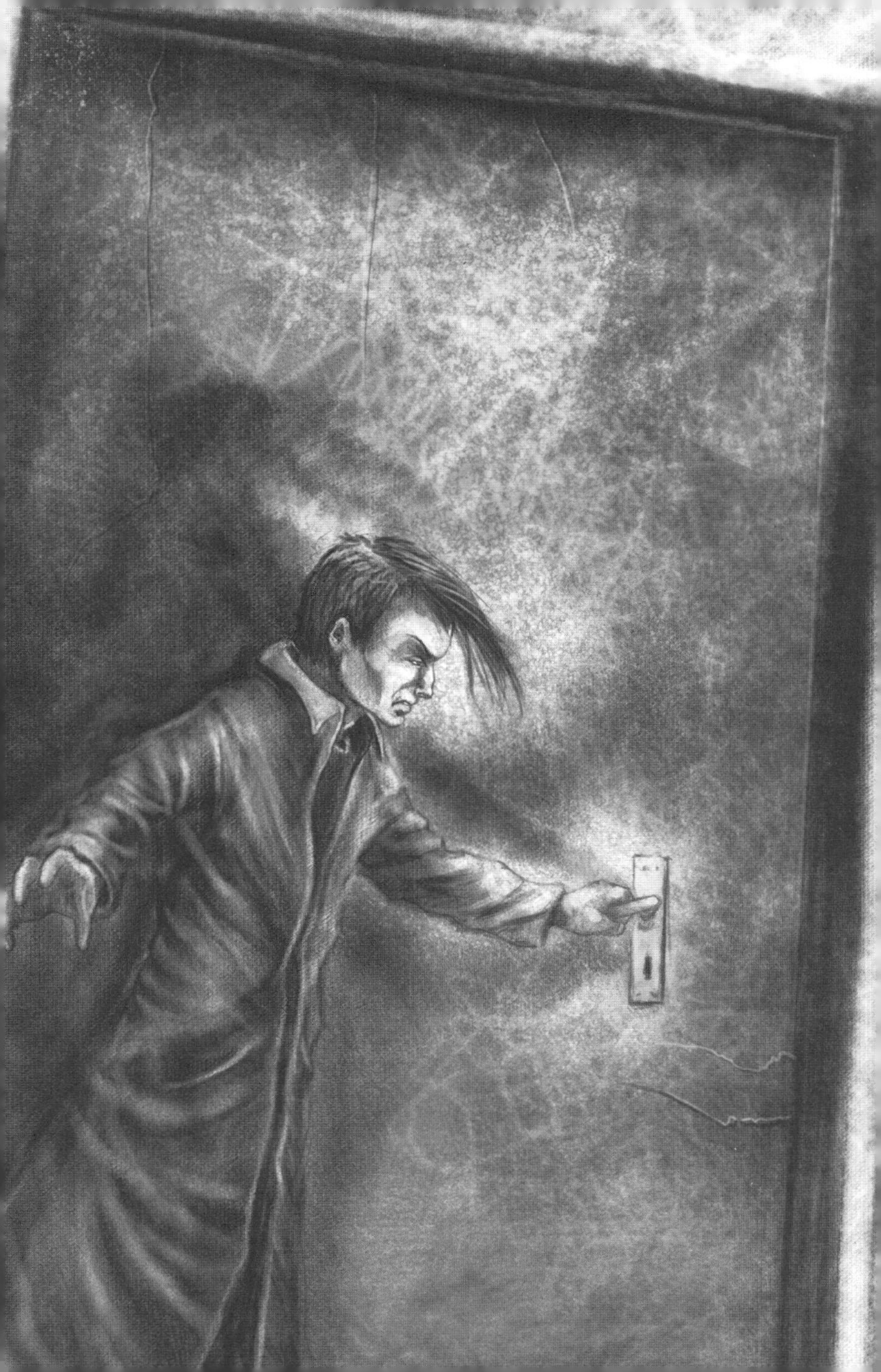

He hears a noise from the far side of the room.

He makes his way over to the sound, and his hands touch a body that he cannot see. He feels a gag in the body's mouth and removes it.

"It's holding me! Pull me free!"

The Dark Man knows the voice.

It is Angela.

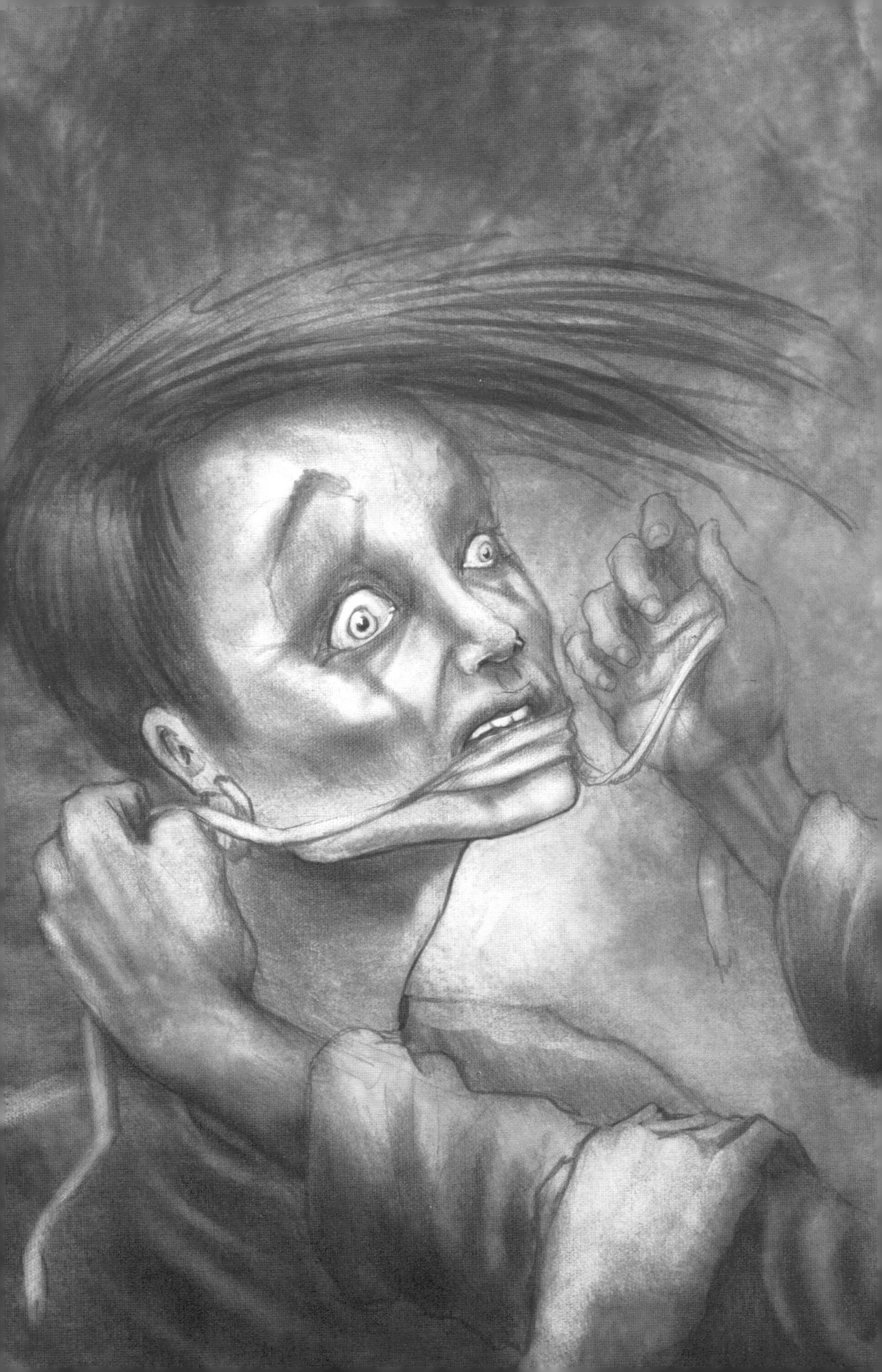

"What is holding you?" he asks.

"The darkness!" she hisses. "It's alive! Pull me free. We have to get out of here!"

The Dark Man grabs her shoulders. He tries to pull her free, but something resists.

"Pull harder!" Angela insists.

The Dark Man pulls her sharply, and she breaks free. They tumble to the ground.

"Quick," Angela says. "Let's go. It will hold us here if it can!"

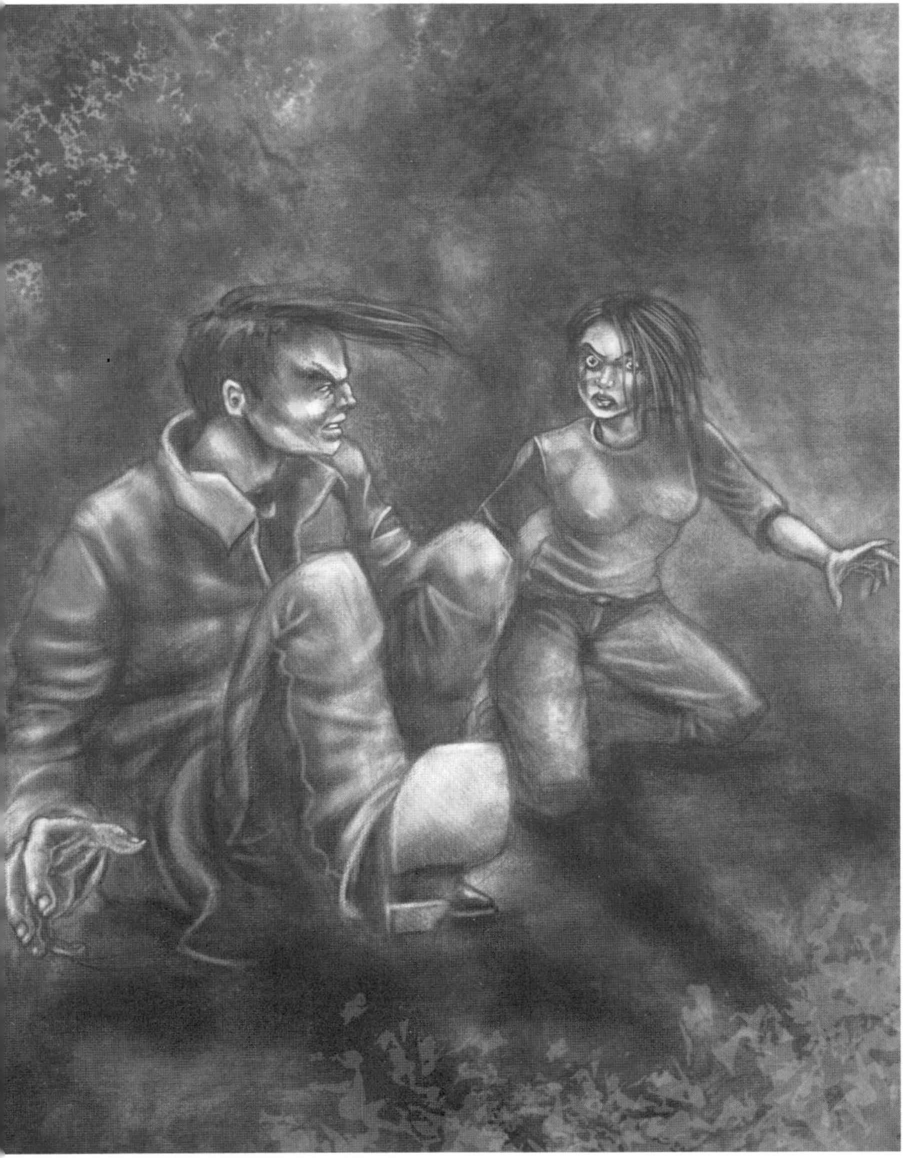

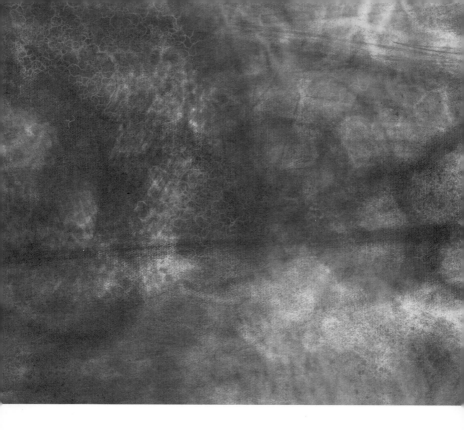

The Dark Man grabs Angela's hand and rushes back to where he hopes the door is.

They crash against it. The Dark Man opens the door, and they tumble into the corridor.

It is dark here, but at least they can see.

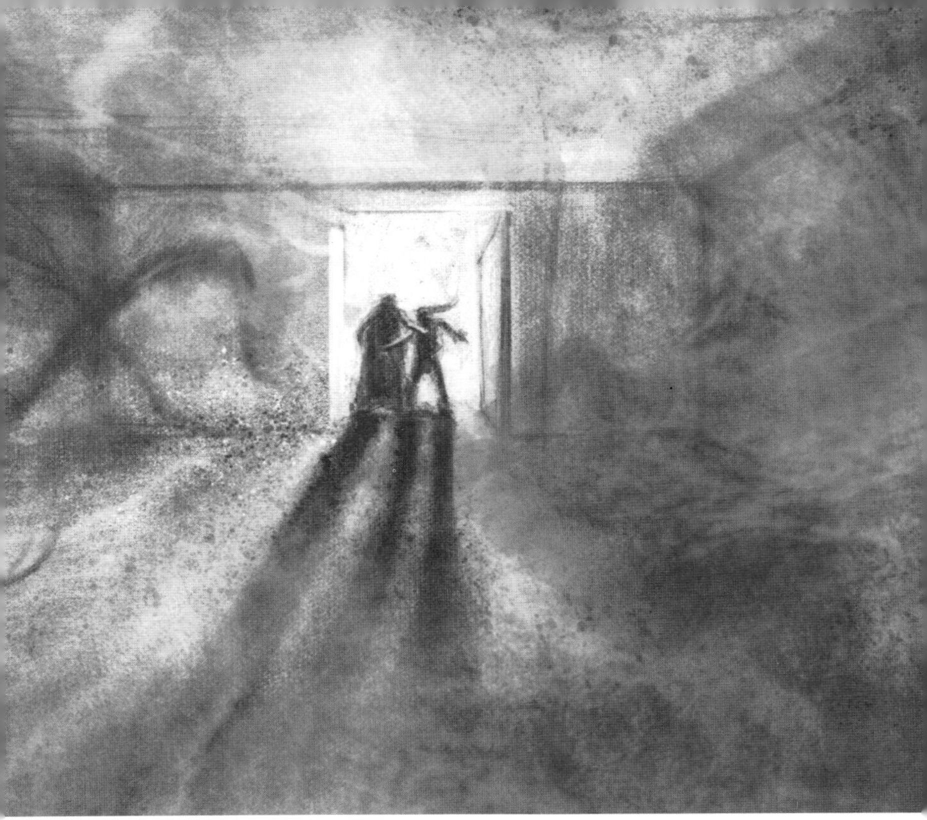

As they run, the Dark Man looks back.

It seems as though light is streaming in through the open door. From inside the room comes a noise like a strangled scream.

The light is destroying the darkness.

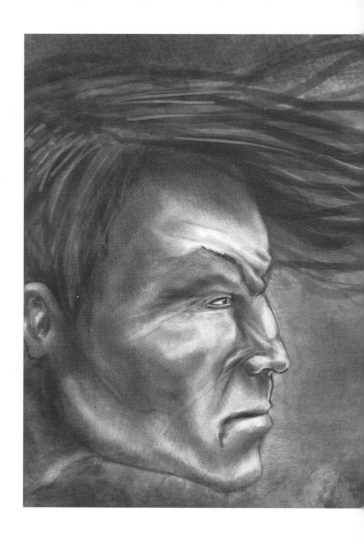

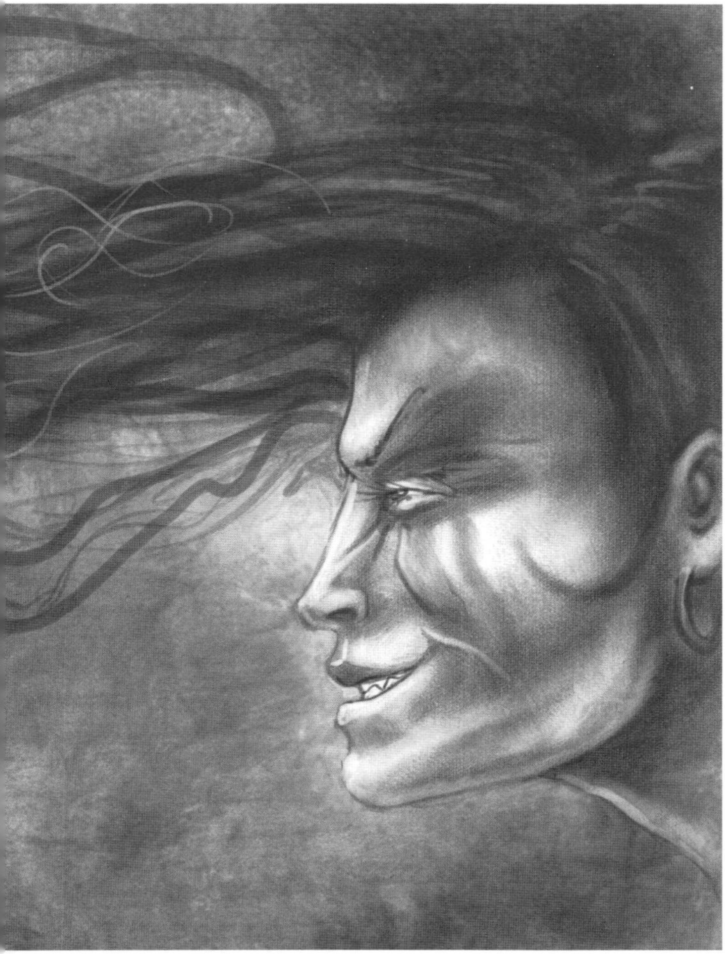

When they are safe, Angela turns to face the Dark Man. Her smile is wicked.

“Who would have thought that you would be my hero?” she says.

The Dark Man shakes his head. "The Old Man asked me to rescue you," he says.

Angela shrugs. "Well, it was worth it," she says. "I saw something in the darkness back there."

"Yes? What?"

"The Golden Cup is back," Angela replies, "and I can tell you where it is.

"But you'll have to wait until tomorrow. I have plans for tonight."

She turns and heads towards the elevators,
where the little boy is waiting.

The Dark Man sees how she looks at the boy,
so he starts to follow her.

No one is ever safe around Angela.

THE AUTHOR

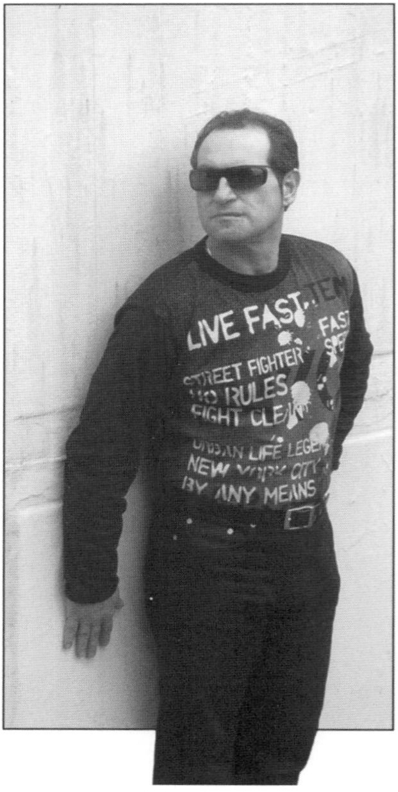
LIVE FAST
STREET FIGHTER
RULES
BY ANY MEANS

photograph: Rachel Ottewill

Peter Lancett is a writer, fiction editor, and film maker living and working in New Zealand and sometimes Los Angeles. He claims that one day he'll "settle down and get a proper job."